CW01020169

PINGU

Feels Left Out

BBC CHILDREN'S BOOKS

One day Pingu spotted his
friends Robby the seal and
Pengi playing badminton
together.

"Hi there!" shouted Pingu.

The badminton game looked great fun.

"Can I have a go?" Pingu asked, reaching out for a racket.

"Not now," said Pengi. "I'm just getting into my stride. Go and ask Robby."

But Robby wouldn't let Pingu have a go either.
"I'll just play for a little bit longer," said Robby.
"Why don't you sit and watch us?"

Pingu walked away. He felt a bit left out, especially as Robby was really *his* special friend, not Pengi's.

"I'll watch for a bit," he thought to himself. "Then I'll make sure they let me play."

Pingu went and stood nearby. Right next to him was a big basket of fish.

"What a stroke of luck," he exclaimed. He began to reach into the basket for something to eat while he watched the game of badminton.

Suddenly Pingu was startled by a
booming voice.

"Hey!" shouted Pengi, fiercely.

"Leave that fish alone. It's ours.
Go and sit further away."

"All right, all right," said Pingu, moving away.
When they weren't looking he added, "Meanies!"
and stuck his tongue out at them.

The game of badminton seemed to go on and on. Pingu stood and watched the shuttlecock fly endlessly back and forth from Robby to Pengi. He felt bored and miserable.

Then Pengi gave the shuttlecock a huge *whack* and sent it soaring up in the air, high above Robby's head. Robby watched as it went sailing off towards Pingu.

It landed just above Pingu on a large block of ice. Pingu looked up at the shuttlecock and suddenly had a brilliant idea.

Pingu climbed quickly to the top of the block of ice and picked up the shuttlecock.

"Ha, ha!" he chuckled, looking down at Robby and Pengi. "Who's got the shuttlecock now?"

"Give it back, Pingu!" shouted Pengi, desperately.
"We'll do anything you want, if you let us have it back," pleaded Robby.

"I'll swap it for that basket of fish down there," Pingu told them. "The whole basket."

14

Pingu produced a coil of rope and threw one end of it down to his friends.

"Attach the basket to the end of rope and then I can haul it up," he ordered.

But Pengi wasn't going to let Pingu get the better of them like this. He had already thought of a plan to trick Pingu and he whispered it to Robby. Robby liked playing tricks and he began to chuckle when he heard it.

Meanwhile Pingu was beginning to cheer up. Things were definitely going his way now. He put the shuttlecock on his head and whistled away while he waited for his friends to do as he said.

Pingu couldn't see that his two friends were up to mischief. Robby dived into a hole in the ice and came up with a large crab! He slid it along the ground to Pengi.

Pengi caught it in the fish basket and then placed the fish on top so that Pingu wouldn't notice it. He attached the basket to the end of rope so that it was all ready for Pingu to pull up.

"Pull away, Pingu," shouted Pengi.

Pingu pulled and pulled. Up came the basket of fish. "That's it," said Pingu, grabbing hold of the heavy basket and placing it beside him.

"Here's your silly old shuttlecock," Pingu shouted as he dropped it back down to his friends. "I'd rather have a basket of fish any day."

But as soon as Pingu put his hand into the basket the crab caught hold of him with its sharp claws.

"OUCH!" yelled Pingu. He fell backwards off the block of ice.

It was all too much for Pingu. His hand hurt and his friends were being horrid to him. He sat at the foot of the block of ice and cried.

Robby was sorry that he and Pengi had been so mean to Pingu. He went rushing up and stroked Pingu's sore hand.

"We'll go and get you some fish from the basket to make you feel better," he said, soothingly.

But Pengi started to eat the fish from the basket himself. One after the other he tossed the fish into his mouth and gobbled them up.

"Hey!" cried Robby. "Slow down or there won't be any left for Pingu."

Robby was right. In a short while the two friends looked in the basket and found only one small fish left.

"Oh, dear!" said Pengi. "I didn't realise I'd eaten quite so many."

Robby and Pengi looked
guiltily down at Pingu.
    "Poor Pingu," said Robby,
beginning to cry.
    "I shouldn't have been so
greedy," sighed Pengi.

27

Robby and Pengi gave Pingu the one remaining fish. Pingu cheered up at once and so did Robby when he saw Pingu happily munching away.

"How about a game of badminton now?" Pengi asked Pingu.

"That's just what I feel like," said Pingu, taking Robby's racket.

So all three of them played badminton together.
Robby managed to use his tail as a racket which
made them all laugh.

"Badminton is a great game," said Pingu. "And it's a lot more fun playing together than watching!"

More delightful Pingu stories to read and favourite characters to collect

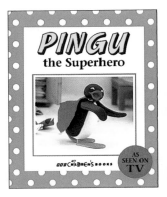

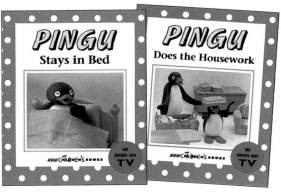

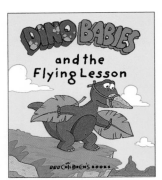

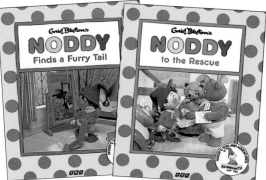

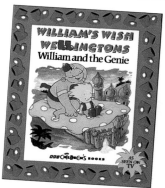

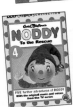

Pingu magazine every month
Make learning fun!

BBC CHILDREN'S PUBLISHING